SONY PICTURES
ANIMATION

CON⏻NECTED

The Mitchells'
FAMILY ROAD TRIP!
(Or That Time They Saved the World)

Adapted by Patty Michaels • Illustrated by Tiffany Lam

SIMON SPOTLIGHT
An imprint of Simon & Schuster Children's Publishing Division
New York   London   Toronto   Sydney   New Delhi

1230 Avenue of the Americas, New York, New York 10020 • This Simon Spotlight paperback edition September 2020 • TM & © 2020 Sony Pictures Animation Inc.
All Rights Reserved. All rights reserved, including the right of reproduction in whole or in part in any form. SIMON SPOTLIGHT and colophon are
registered trademarks of Simon & Schuster, Inc. For information about special discounts for bulk purchases, please contact Simon & Schuster Special Sales at
1-866-506-1949 or business@simonandschuster.com. Manufactured in the United States of America 0720 LAK • 10 9 8 7 6 5 4 3 2 1
ISBN 978-1-5344-7600-4 • ISBN 978-1-5344-7601-1 (eBook)

Hey, I'm Katie. This is my mom, dad, and little brother, Aaron. We just got back from our road trip.

Oh, and we also saved the world from a robot takeover! It all started when I was just about to go away to college. . . .

Dad decided that we were going to take a family road trip so that we could be together as a family, instead of me flying to school solo.

Bummer! I knew I would miss out on so many cool things happening at school already.

I tried to make the best of it. At least I could shoot some footage and make a cool video!

Making movies was my favorite thing to do. Especially when our dog, Monchi, was the star!

Check out some of these cool movie posters I made!

Now, back to our road trip. My brother, Aaron, was super excited to visit Dino Stop. Although he didn't think the dinosaurs looked accurate at *all*.

It was at Dino Stop when we realized that robots were *actually* trying to take over the world. But we are the Mitchells! These robots weren't going to defeat us.

My dad's idea was to build this giant barricade to keep us safe from the robots. He wanted to use his survival skills to protect us.

But those weren't his only skills. Let's not forget about his super fancy driving move he calls "The Rick Mitchell Special." He can even sing while doing it!

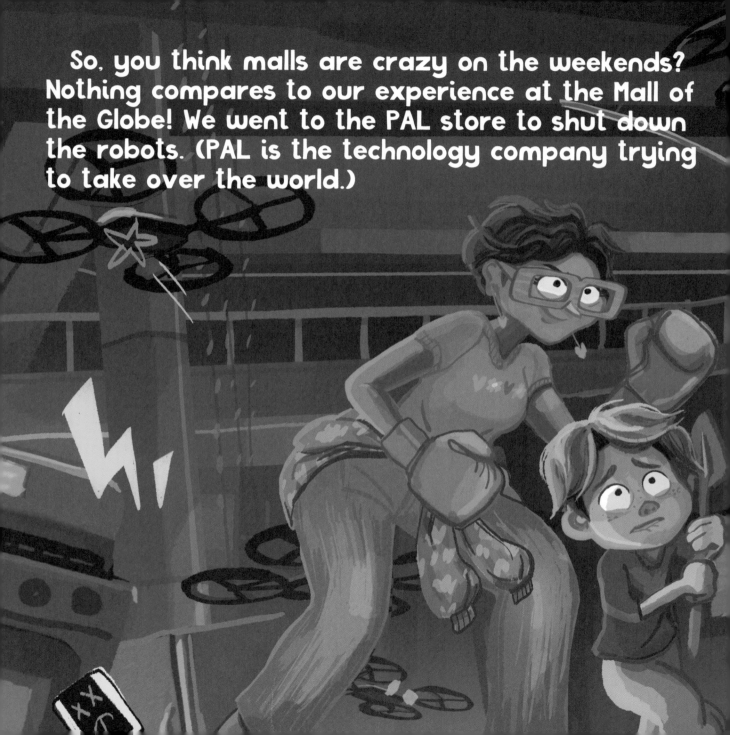

So, you think malls are crazy on the weekends? Nothing compares to our experience at the Mall of the Globe! We went to the PAL store to shut down the robots. (PAL is the technology company trying to take over the world.)

But everything started to attack us! (Toys, microwaves, toasters—you name it!) It turned out PAL was controlling everything with a Wi-Fi signal!

But guess what? We learned that not *all* robots are dangerous. Introducing our new friends . . . Eric and Deborahbot 5000! They were defective robots who became damaged during one of the robot battles. They turned out to be really cool.

And they gave us the secret code that would stop the tech rising . . . forever!

In the end it was up to us to save the world.
And by working together as a family, we did it!

So, that about wraps up our crazy adventure. Now I'm off to college. Although I'm excited about my new school, I'm really going to miss my family. They are my people.